W9-CQW-341

LET'S COUNT
the PUPPIES

LET'S COUNT the PUPPIES

Katharine Kunhardt

KATHERINE TEGEN BOOKS
An Imprint of HarperCollinsPublishers

Here is **1** puppy waving hello.
He's so happy to see you.

1 black pup and 1 yellow pup make 2 puppies in a wreath.

Peekaboo!

Can you count the puppies?

1, 2, 3!

Here are **4** puppies

playing follow the leader.

How many puppies are in
this big round kettle?

5.

Yes!

6 black puppies
are about to learn
some tricks.

6

Can you make
them sit?
And shake hands?

7 puppies play house.
Would you like to play, too?

8 hungry puppies
make a circle.
What are they doing?
They are eating
their supper.

Look!
9 little puppies wait for a bath.

1, 2, 3, 4, 5, 6, 7, 8, 9, 10!

10 puppies are running
in the snow.

Mommy dog is feeding her **11** puppies.

12 puppies are sitting on a bench.

They want
to say bye-bye.

12

Bye-bye.

FROM MY SCRAPBOOK

When my six children grew up, I decided it was time to have some puppies. We'd always had dogs, but up until then we hadn't bred them. In the past twenty-five years, though, my dogs have had 162 puppies! They've all been Labrador retrievers. I like Labs because they are big, soft, gentle, and smart, and they love children. Since I have seventeen grandchildren now who all love to play with them, that is important. Most of the puppies go to new homes, but I sometimes keep one, so that we always have four dogs. They sleep in the bedroom with my husband and me. We live outside of New York City, but in the summer we all go to Maine, where we own a little island. I think our Labs are happiest there. They like to run on the rocks, swim, sit on the sand, and look out over the ocean—pretending they are little puppies again.

—*Katharine Kunhardt*

My first dog, Abby, with her daughter Samantha

Sophie in the long grass

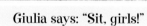
Giulia says: "Sit, girls!"

Creedence on the sand spit

Kate, Sophie, and Lily on Crow Island

Kate wishes she were sailing

Samantha and Abby

Peter, George, Abby, and Teddy with pups

Sophie and her daughter Ceci

Ear-flapping boat ride

Our newest addition to the
family—Kate's daughter Annie

For my dearest Phil

Let's Count the Puppies   Copyright © 2004 by Katharine Kunhardt
Manufactured in China by South China Printing Company Ltd. All rights reserved.
www.harperchildrens.com

Library of Congress Cataloging-in-Publication Data
Kunhardt, Katharine.   Let's count the puppies / Katharine Kunhardt.—1st ed.   p. cm.
Summary: Photographs of Labrador retriever puppies playing and eating help the reader learn to count to twelve.
ISBN: 0-06-054336-1 — ISBN 0-06-054337-X (lib. bdg.)
1. Counting— Juvenile literature. [1. Counting. 2. Labrador retriever. 3. Animals—Infancy.] I. Title.
QA113.K86 2004   513.2'11—dc21   2002152942   CIP   AC

1 2 3 4 5 6 7 8 9 10   ❖   First Edition